SNICKERDOODLE TAKES THE CAKE

Ethan Long

Holiday House  New York

Kirby is an early riser.

Snickerdoodle is not. But . . .

Mom's Famous Lemon
Poppy Seed Cake
with Buttercream Icing
always perks
Snickerdoodle up!

But . . .

The note said
"Do Not Touch!"

But . . .

the note does not say
"Do not try one tiny little crumb!"

One little
tiny crumb.

The crumb makes Snickerdoodle's urge for Lemon Poppy Seed Cake with Buttercream Icing hard to resist.

Mom asks, "What's going on out here?",

And . . .

it doesn't take a super
sleuth to figure it out.

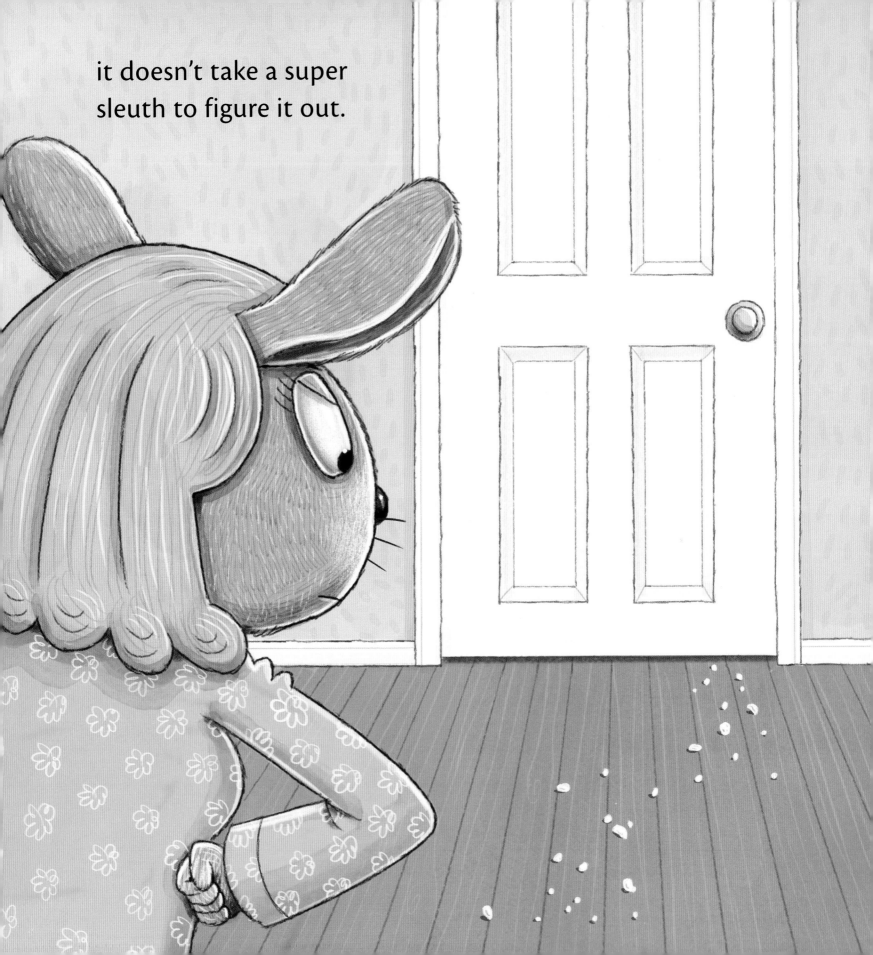

"Get out here and help me fix it!" says Mom.

But it's too late!

Snickerdoodle has a plan.

A few hours later, they spread on the buttercream icing

and they drive to Na Na and Pop Pop's house.

"Oh my! What a beautiful cake!" says Na Na.

Snickerdoodle eats two slices. But . . .

He still wants a little bit more, and . . .

it's delicious!

For Jimmy and Laney

HOLIDAY HOUSE is registered in the U.S. Patent and Trademark Office.

Printed and bound in April 2017 at Hong Kong Graphics and Printing Ltd., China.

The artwork in this book was created using a variety of digital brushes and textures.

First Edition

1 3 5 7 9 10 8 6 4 2

www.holidayhouse.com

Library of Congress Cataloging-in-Publication Data is available.

ISBN 978-0-8234-3784-9

11/21/17